DEFENDERS OF THE GALAXY

The galaxy has many heroes – be they powerful, Force-wielding Jedi Knights, or bold and valiant rebels. But let it never be forgotten that there would be no heroes without their brave assistants!

CABLE CONNECTIONS

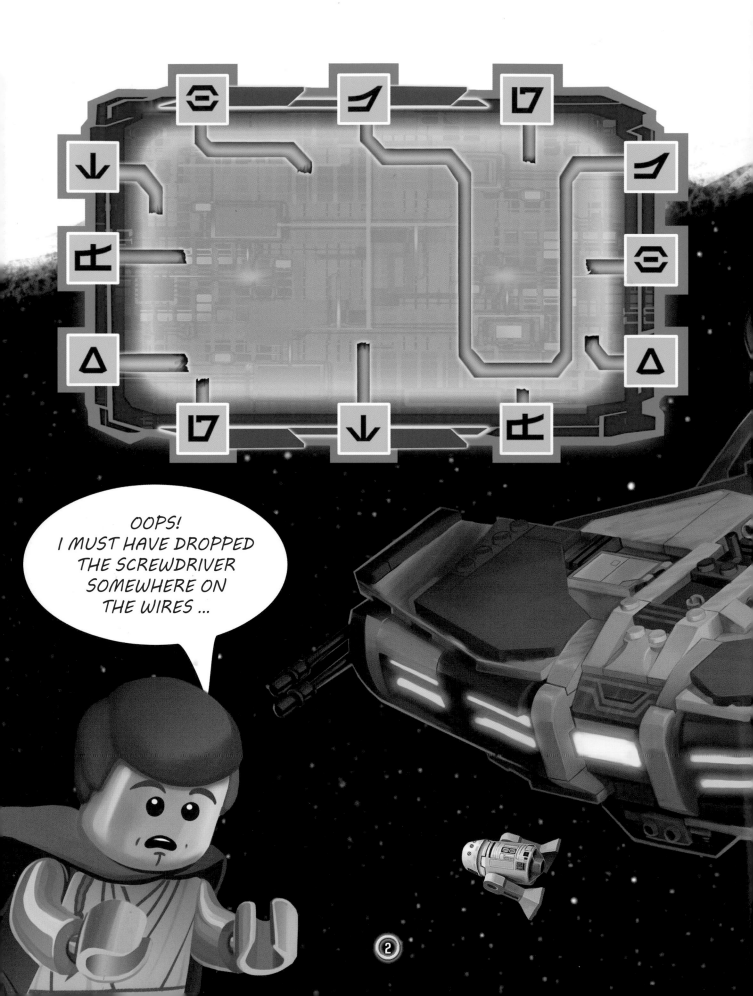

There are three astromech droids struggling to fix this Jedi starship. Help them repair it by drawing lines to fix the wires, making sure the symbols at each end of the wire match.

OH BROTHER, NOT AGAIN! I HOPE ARTOO CAN FIX THEM.

A MIRAGE

After a long, tiresome journey through the hot desert, it was a relief to find Yoda selling lemonade. But was it just a mirage? Look at the small pictures melting in the hot air and mark where they can be found in the big picture.

1   2   3   4

STRONG WITH THE FORCE

ANAKIN, I SENSE A GREAT SENSITIVITY WITH THE FORCE IN YOU!

REALLY?

COULD I CHECK THE MIDI-CHLORIAN COUNT IN YOUR BLOOD?

OH, NO! I HATE NEEDLES!

LISTEN, IT'S REALLY IMPORTANT ...

I DON'T WANT AN INJECTION! I HAVE NO FORCE!

BUT IT'S ONLY A ...

I HAVE NO FORCE, AND YOU DO NOT WANT TO USE THE SYRINGE.

YOU HAVE NO FORCE, AND I DO NOT WANT TO USE THE SYRINGE.

?!!

THE GREAT RACE

Help Anakin Skywalker win the speeder race by finding the shortest way to the finish line. Be quick, the young pilot is revving his engine!

AREN'T YOU A BIT TOO OLD TO PLAY IN THE SAND, MASTER QUI-GON JINN?

FIRST FLIGHT

Anakin launched the starship by guessing the passcode. Look at the three sequences at the bottom of the page. Fill in the final box of each one to work out the passcode.

@#%@%!!!

BUCKLE UP, ARTOO!

ON THE RADAR

Anakin's astromech droid, R2-D2, operates the radar. Help the droid recognise the shadows by drawing lines to connect them with the four matching ships below, then circle the two that don't match.

KNIGHT-IN-TRAINING

When he was younger, Anakin studied at the Jedi Academy. On his first day, he took all his books to his class because he didn't know which ones he would need. C-3PO took this funny photo ...

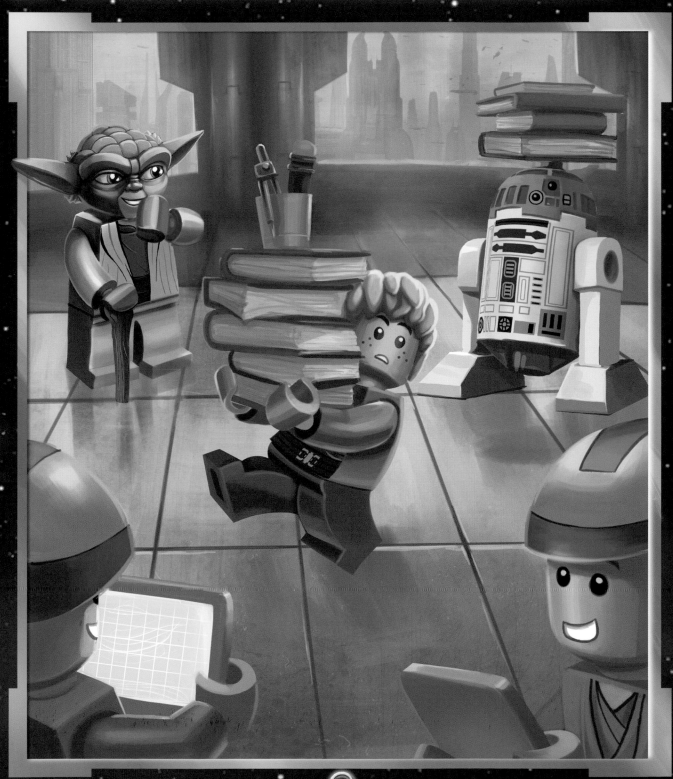

At first glance this photo looks identical to the one on the left. But an expert eye will see eleven differences between them. Find and circle them all.

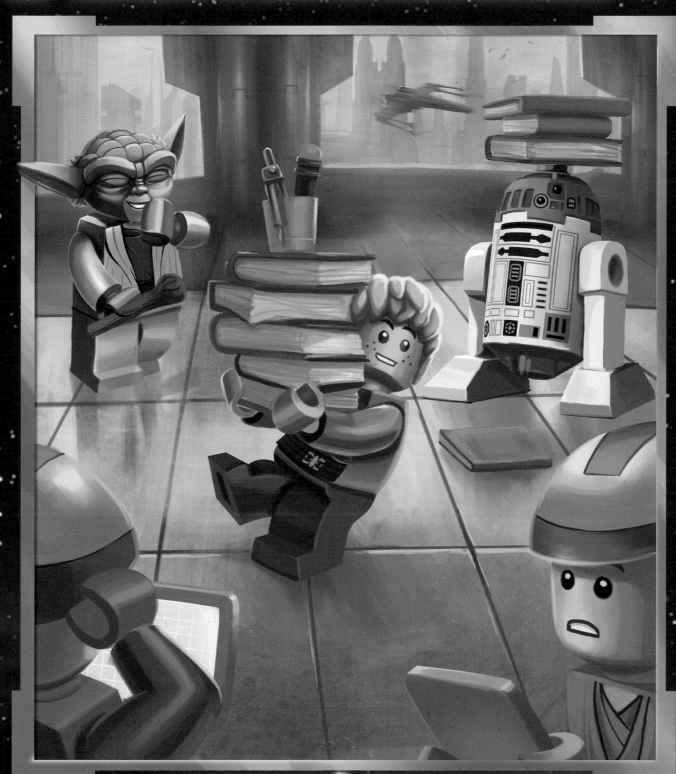

DESERT SEARCH

Anakin Skywalker has lost his trusty droid in the sand dunes! He put a special chip in R2-D2's systems, so he should be able to find him. Look at the map, find the droid's location and write its coordinates in the empty box.

A NEW MODEL

Anakin lost his lightsaber in a duel with Count Dooku. Use the outline below to design a powerful new weapon for the young Jedi Knight, so he can fight the evil Count again.

YOU BREAK IT – YOU PAY FOR IT!

FREE SEATS

There are still spaces left on the transporter. Draw circles in the grid below to add the missing clone troopers. Make sure the number of clones in each row and column matches the number at the end of the row and column they are in. The remaining empty boxes are the free seats!

MASTER VERSUS STUDENT

After joining the dark side, Anakin – now known as Darth Vader – attacked his master, Obi-Wan Kenobi. Draw lines to show where each cut-off piece of the picture should be.

AN UNUSUAL MISSION

DISTORTED HOLOGRAM

R2-D2 found Obi-Wan Kenobi, so he can pass along the encrypted message from Leia Organa. Remove the distortions in the message by numbering the hologram pieces to put them in the right order.

STAR DRILL

The training drill on the Death Star didn't go very well. Look at the battle formations then, starting from the second row down, circle the new trooper that has joined each row.

IF YOU STAND NICELY, THE LEMONADE'S ON ME!

Luke hid his lightsaber in a swamp and left R2-D2 with a note to help him find it. Answer the TRUE or FALSE questions to find the hiding place. When the answer is FALSE follow a red arrow, and when it is TRUE follow a blue arrow.

LUKE SKYWALKER DOESN'T LIKE R2-D2.

ANAKIN SKYWALKER TURNED TO THE DARK SIDE OF THE FORCE.

R2-D2 BROUGHT OBI-WAN KENOBI A SECRET MESSAGE FROM LEIA ORGANA.

YODA IS A WISE BLUE-SKINNED JEDI MASTER.

JEDI KNIGHTS FIGHT WITH LIGHTSABERS.

FULL THROTTLE

Chased by a group of TIE fighters, Han Solo flew the *Millennium Falcon* into an asteroid maze, and now he needs your help to get out! The *Falcon* can only fly over the asteroids with craters to get from the START to the FINISH safely. Draw the route through the maze by connecting all the safe asteroids.

DRESS REHEARSAL

Darth Vader wants to convince his son, Luke Skywalker, to join the dark side. He's practising his speech in front of the mirror. Which two reflections of Vader are identical? There's also a picture with a different item on the mirror shelf. Can you tell which one?

JEDI TRAINING

Luke Skywalker must use the Force to clear the tree trunks off the forest path. Luke can't move a trunk that's lying under another trunk – he must lift the top trunk first. Number the logs in the order the Jedi needs to move them.

FORCE CONSTELLATIONS

The Force is strong in the galaxy. It's even powerful enough to create constellations of great Jedi heroes! Look at the stars and find the constellation that is different from all the others. Which two constellations are identical?

STAR QUIZ

1. Choose the correct name of this Jedi Master:
    a) Qui-Gon Jim
    b) Qui-Gon Jinn
    c) Quin-Gon Jin

2. What kind of droid is R2-D2?
    a) protocol droid
    b) medical droid
    c) astromech droid

3. What starships are used to move troopers across the galaxy?
    a) transporters
    b) starfighters
    c) tankers

4. Who was Anakin Skywalker's Jedi Master?
    a) Yoda
    b) Mace Windu
    c) Obi-Wan Kenobi

5. A hologram is used to:
   a) detect the influence of the dark side
   b) pass along information
   c) cool rooms

6. Who was the captain of the *Millennium Falcon*?
   a) Han Solo
   b) Chewbacca
   c) Luke Skywalker

7. What name did Anakin Skywalker take after turning to the dark side of the Force?
   a) Luke
   b) Vader
   c) Sidious

ANSWERS

Pg. 2 CABLE CONNECTIONS

Pg. 4 A MIRAGE

Pg. 6-7 THE GREAT RACE

Pg. 8 FIRST FLIGHT

Pg. 9 ON THE RADAR

Pg. 10-11 KNIGHT-IN-TRAINING

Pg. 12 DESERT SEARCH

E-2

Pg. 14 FREE SEATS

Pg. 15 MASTER VERSUS STUDENT

Pg. 18 DISTORTED HOLOGRAM

Pg. 19 STAR DRILL

Pg. 20-21 LIGHTSABER SEARCH

Pg. 22-23 FULL THROTTLE

Pg. 24 DRESS REHEARSAL

Pg. 25 JEDI TRAINING

Pg. 26-27 FORCE CONSTELLATIONS

Pg. 28-29 STAR QUIZ

1 – b, 2 – c, 3 – a, 4 – c,
5 – b, 6 – a, 7 – b.

HOW TO BUILD R2-D2